GILBERT

THE GREEN-EYED RABBIT

GILBERT

THE GREEN-EYED RABBIT

DR. POPPY

XULON ELITE

Xulon Press Elite
2301 Lucien Way #415
Maitland, FL 32751
407.339.4217
www.xulonpress.com

Paperback ISBN-13: 978-1-6628-4449-2
Ebook ISBN-13: 978-1-6628-4450-8

Content

Gilbert the Green-Eyed Rabbit

BY
POPPY

Now most people know that rabbits have either brown or pink eyes. It all depends on if they're a wild rabbit or a domestic rabbit, like the kind you get at Easter. Well, not too deep in the woods, a little, wild rabbit was born. He was one of a litter of nine that lived in a burrow under an oak tree. This little rabbit spent his first few days snuggled up against his mommy's nice, warm fur. He didn't want to leave his warm home-made bed, but it wasn't long before his mommy led him and his brothers and sisters outside and into another warm place, though it was a lot brighter! There were great smells and lots to see, and he couldn't wait to stretch his legs and try out a few hops. But Mommy said it wasn't safe to just run around outside their home-you had to watch for danger, like foxes and hawks!

Every day, Gilbert—that's the name proudly given to him by his mommy—carefully went to the edge of the tunnel and peeked outside. He sniffed the air, looked up to the sky, and hopped outside. Now on one especially warm and sunny day, he sniffed the grass as he hopped from his home, and it smelled good enough to eat!

Gilbert carefully licked a blade of grass. It tasted okay, so he nibbled a little more … and a little more, and a little more. Soon he had eaten a belly full. Boy, did he feel good as he laid down in the warm sun. He hadn't been outside for more than an hour when he heard his mommy call. "Gilbert! Make quick like a bunny and get back home!" she said in a squeaky voice. She always sounded like that when there was danger. "Hurry, Gilbert! I hear sounds!"

With that, Gilbert heard them too! He tried to run, but he had eaten too much grass, and his belly was full. He hopped and hopped as fast as he could, and the sounds grew louder. Just as he got to the edge of his home, he saw what made the noise. It was a human boy, one of those big creatures that had made their home on the other side of the pasture, a good ten minutes of hopping from his. Gilbert hurried down the tunnel and snuggled up close to his mommy, along with all his brothers and sisters. They waited for the sound to go away, and while they waited, Gilbert fell fast asleep.

When Gilbert woke up, it was dark, and everyone had gone outside again, including his mommy. Gilbert decided to join them. He really liked the grass he had eaten and looked forward to trying other things to eat as well. Just a short distance from his home, he found a new plant, and it looked like it might taste really good! Its leaves weren't tall and thin like the grass he had eaten. These leaves were small and round, and you could eat them all the way down to the ground. Just then, Mommy came hopping over and said, "Gilbert, that's clover! You shouldn't eat too much, or it'll make your eyes green!"

But Gilbert was hungry, and he just laughed and laughed and went on nibbling the clover. Well, it wasn't long before his belly began to hurt from so much clover. He didn't feel so good, and he carefully hopped back to his home, went down the tunnel, curled up, and fell fast asleep.

Well, the next morning, when his mommy woke him to go outside, he blinked his sleepy eyes and heard his mommy shout, "Oh no! You ate too much clover, Gilbert! It turned your eyes green!" Gilbert thought about having green eyes, but he didn't know much about colors anyway. So he happily hopped outside to be with his brothers and sisters-and to eat more clover! All his siblings saw him and noticed that his eyes were green. He looked different, they thought, but he smelled like Gilbert. What were they to do? So they all hopped away, and poor Gilbert had no-one to play with or eat clover with.

He was sad. Still, he ate more and more clover. His belly grew bigger, and his legs grew stronger. He hopped higher, and his cotton grew longer, but his eye color remained green. His mommy still loved him, green eyes and all.

Gilbert kept eating the grass and clover near his house, and it wasn't long before there wasn't much left. So Gilbert hopped a little further away from his home, all the way across the back of the meadow to the funny looking path with metal rails running through it. His mommy had warned him about this place and told him to stay away from it. There was a huge monster that belched smoke and rang bells and had those human people on it! But the clover and grass grew all around there, and he didn't have to share with his brothers and sisters!

It wasn't long before his mommy called him, "Gilbert! Gilbert, get away from there! You get back to the house right now!" Gilbert just laughed and slowly hopped back to his mommy.

"Gilbert, you better listen! I'll tell you a story about a little worm that didn't pay attention." And with that, all the bunnies gathered around Mommy and listened to the story. "Ooey Gooey was a worm, a little worm was he. He sat upon the railroad track, a train he did not see!"

Now, Mommy often told stories like that to make learning fun. Gilbert said, "Mommy, tell us another please!"

So Mommy began again. "A peanut sat on the railroad track, waiting for his mother. A train came whistling by real fast. Oops! Now he's peanut butter!"

Well, it was time for bed, and Mommy tucked in all nine bunnies. It was getting crowded with all of the bunnies growing, and it wouldn't be long before Gilbert and his siblings would go and make their own homes. But for now, they all fell asleep, and Gilbert dreamed about all of the grass and clover he would eat the next day by the railroad tracks.

Well, the morning sun shined down the hole, and one by one the bunnies hopped out into the bright sunshine. Gilbert hopped out last. He knew where he was going for breakfast!

Right across the meadow to the train tracks he hopped. Now, he knew his mommy wouldn't approve, but he would only stay for a short time.

Gilbert quickly hopped right up to the tracks and looked around. He didn't see any danger, so he started to eat and eat and eat. He ate all of the grass and clover alongside of the tracks and looked over the rail. Boy, did that grass look good between the tracks!

But Mommy said don't go there! He looked around again, wriggled his nose, sniffed the air, and hopped over the track and began to eat. He ate so much grass and clover that his green eyes began to feel tired. "Why not take a nap here?" he thought. He laid down right between the train tracks and fell asleep.

Gilbert was napping for a very long time when suddenly, that great big monster roared down the tracks toward him. It was belching smoke and big clouds of steam and making a horrible racket. Gilbert woke with a start. His green eyes were wide open from fear. His legs were shaking, and he couldn't make his legs hop fast enough to get out of the way! He shook with fear, and in a flash, the horrible noise-making monster was right over the top of him! The ground shook, and it got dark as the monster roared over him. Poor Gilbert was so afraid that he backed up against the track, and his big, fluffy cotton tail stuck out. In a flash, the wheel of the monster ran over part of his tail!

"Ouch! That hurt!" Gilbert cried, and the monster roared away. Gilbert hopped as fast as he could back across the meadow and all the way to his home. "Mommy! Mommy!" he cried, big bunny tears rolling down his fat cheeks. "Mommy, My tail's gone!" said Gilbert.

"Well," said Mommy. "I told you not to go there, and now you're missing part of your tail! Gilbert, you must listen to me," said Mommy. "It's better to only be missing part of your cotton tail than to not be here at all! Maybe, with some luck, your tail will grow back. But you can't go near there ever again!" As Gilbert snuggled up next to his mommy where he felt safe and warm, he knew he'd listen from now on. Mommies know best! Gilbert fell fast asleep.

Gilbert Meets the Twins Next Door

BY
POPPY

As Gilbert carefully peeked out of the burrow one day, he heard strange sounds coming from the field nearby. *"Bah!"* went the sound. *"Bah, Bah, Bah!"* he heard. He had to see what was making the noise! It didn't sound like any creature that he was friends with.

Gilbert carefully hopped toward the sounds and sniffed the air with his little, pink nose and watched the sky with his big, green eyes. The strange sounds continued. After a few more hops, he came to the edge of the field, and he saw two strange looking animals. They were eating the grass in the field, and every once in a while, one of them would stop and cry out, *"Bah!"*

Now, Gilbert had never been told about such animals by his mother, so he didn't know if there was danger here, but he had to get closer to see what these funny looking animals were! He carefully hopped closer for a better look. They looked like big, fluffy balls of cotton, and one was colored black-as black as his den was at night, while the other was as white as snow.

"*Bah!*" said the black colored animal as it stopped eating grass and looked at Gilbert. "*Bah!*" it said again, and the funny looking animal slowly walked over to where Gilbert had laid down. They sniffed each other with their noses. Gilbert didn't think that there was any danger, so he stayed still and let the animal continue to inspect him.

After a minute, Gilbert said, "Hi, I'm Gilbert. What's your name?"

"Well," said the animal. "I'm Kevin, and I'm a lamb. What are you?"

"I'm a bunny, and I live over in the brambles next to the edge of the field! Do you like grass as much as I do?"

Kevin said, "I sure do! My sister, Kaleigh, loves grass too! Come with me, and you can meet her."

Gilbert and Kevin went over to meet Kaleigh, who had a big bunch of grass in her mouth. Quickly, she chewed it, swallowed it with a gulp, and said, "*Bah!* Hello, I'm Kaleigh, and I'm Kevin's sister. We just moved here a few days ago, and that nice boy, Christopher, brings us out here to eat grass and play."

"Well, I know Christopher too! He plays with me sometimes," said Gilbert. "We hop around in the grass and run and jump. Does Christopher play like that with you too?" asked Gilbert to his new friends.

"Yes, he does," said Kevin. "He can jump almost as high as I can! Watch!" With that, Kevin jumped straight up in the air!

"Wow!" said Gilbert. "You can really jump high! Now watch me!" Gilbert ran a few steps and jumped as high as he could.

"Hey, you jumped really high for such a little guy!" said Kaleigh. This character is named after my grand daughter and this is how her name is spelled. WB

"Let's jump and play, we've got all day!"

And so, for the rest of the day, Gilbert, Kevin, and Kaleigh jumped, played, and ate grass until it was almost dark.

Gilbert knew it was time to go, so he said goodbye to his two new friends. They promised to meet again the next day for more playtime. Gilbert carefully hopped back toward the edge of the field, stopping every once in a while to sniff the air and look up in the sky.

He found his burrow deep in the thicket and carefully went down where he was met by all of his family. He told everyone about the two new friends he had made, and as he snuggled up next to his mother to go to sleep, he dreamed about his new friends, the warm sunshine, and the wonderful tasting grass. Gilbert smiled as his dreams were happy ones.

We must listen to our parents as they wish to protect us from harm and evil. WB

Gilbert Meets the Boy Across the Meadow

BY
POPPY

Gilbert the green-eyed bunny rabbit hopped out of his burrow and sniffed the fresh air. It was a beautiful spring day, and the sun shone and felt good on his fur. There was plenty of tasty, green clover to eat, and he could hardly wait to carefully hop across the meadow to eat his breakfast. None of his brothers or sisters were to be found, and he didn't see his mommy, so Gilbert decided to make the trip all by himself

As he hopped along, he'd stop and sniff the air and listen carefully for any strange sounds, just like his mommy had taught him. He didn't hear anything but the chirping of some birds and the chatter from a squirrel, so Gilbert hopped along and looked forward to the tasty clover. It took him almost ten minutes to hop across the meadow, and he stopped just a few feet away from the clover to take one last look around. You see, Mommy had warned him about the foxes that lived nearby. It was a big fox that had chased his daddy, and no one had seen his daddy since!

Gilbert's mommy said, "Foxes aren't nice to rabbits. They try to catch us and make us their dinner, so you'd better watch out!" Gilbert remembered what happened to his cotton tail from not listening to his mommy, so he kept looking around and sniffing the air, just like Mommy taught him.

Well, he started to eat the clover, and did it ever taste good! He ate and ate and hopped a few feet, stopped, and ate some more. The sun shined down and made him feel warm and a little sleepy. So Gilbert hopped over to a large sticker bush and carefully crawled inside. "Mr. Fox can't get me in here," he thought. He curled up for a quick nap and quickly went to sleep.

There was a little boy that lived on this side of the meadow, and he was about four or five years old. His mommy called him "Christopher," and she taught him to be kind to animals and never to scare them or throw rocks or sticks at them. Christopher liked animals and had a pet dog and two cats, and he sometimes found lost frogs in his swimming pool. He once found a turtle in his swimming pool and helped the turtle out of the pool and back to the meadow. Christopher's mommy even took him to the zoo to see the big animals, but he was sad to see them locked up in cages looking sad.

But on this beautiful, sunny morning, Christopher was just happy to see the birds flying overhead and hear the squirrels chattering away up in the trees. He really liked to play soccer, but none of his friends were outside yet, so he kicked the soccer ball as far as he could and happily ran after it. As Christopher ran up to the soccer ball, he kicked it as hard as he could, and it went really far, all the way to the edge of the meadow, right up to a big sticker bush. The soccer ball went into the bush, and out popped a little bunny rabbit. He looked frightened, and he just hopped around in circles, not sure where to run. Christopher called, "Hey, little bunny! Don't be afraid, I won't hurt you!"

Well, Gilbert didn't know what to think! One minute he was taking a nap, and the next thing he knew, there was a big crash, branches falling on him, and now there was this strange looking, funny smelling monster making noises. Where was his mommy? What should he do? This big animal didn't seem to be dangerous. "He doesn't look like a fox or smell like a fox … maybe he could play with me!" thought Gilbert. He decided to wait and see what this big animal would do next.

Christopher continued to softly talk to the bunny, and he didn't move or try to touch him. The bunny didn't move, he just remained ready to hop away at any moment. So Christopher carefully sat down a few feet away from the bunny and spoke to him softly. The bunny looked at Christopher, wiggled his nose, and smelled the air. Christopher picked some of the clover and slowly put the clover down in front of the bunny. The bunny sniffed the clover and carefully ate some of it.

Gilbert ate the clover his new friend had picked for him, and it tasted good! Maybe they could share the clover, and afterwards, they could hop around like he did with his brothers and sisters! So Gilbert began to eat some clover, and Christopher gave him some more. It wasn't long before they began to trust each other, and Christopher reached out and let Gilbert smell his hand.

Christopher began to pet Gilbert and scratch him between his ears, and it felt good! They were buddies, and Gilbert started to hop around in circles with Christopher hopping right along behind him. They hopped and hopped for a long time, and they really enjoyed each other's company. Christopher liked this green-eyed bunny rabbit and was glad to find a new friend.

It was then that Christopher's mommy called for him. "Christopher! Christopher, where are you? Come on home now, it's lunchtime!" she said.

Christopher said, "See you later, bunny!" He waved goodbye to his new friend and quickly ran home to eat his lunch.

Gilbert watched as his new friend ran across the meadow, and he knew it was time for him to hop back to his home as well. When the sun is high in the sky, you can't see hawks flying above. This was a dangerous time to be out, so he sniffed the air, listened for strange sounds, and quickly hopped back across the meadow to his burrow. Gilbert was glad to see his brothers and sisters outside, and he stopped to tell them about his big adventure.

With that, he climbed down the tunnel, curled up in a little, furry ball, and went to sleep. He dreamed about his new friend and the fun they had.

Gilbert and the Ugly Worm

BY
POPPY

G ilbert the green-eyed bunny rabbit hopped out of his burrow and sniffed the fresh air. It was early summer, and the days were getting longer, and the grass grew taller and sweeter.

On this particular day, Gilbert had eaten his fill of tasty green grass and clover and was sitting in the warm sunshine that filtered into the briar patch when he saw a little movement up on one of the branches in front of him. Why, it was a worm of some kind! At least, it looked like a worm, but it had legs up front, no legs in the middle, and legs at the back end. On its head it had two fuzzy antennas sticking out in the middle of its wrinkled top.

As Gilbert watched this weird worm, he carefully sniffed the air to see if it had a smell. "Hey, you!" shouted Gilbert. "What kind of worm are you?" The worm just kept inching along the branch as if he was in a big hurry. "Hey, little worm! Where are you going?" asked Gilbert. But the worm inched along, heading toward some big leaves.

Gilbert carefully crept up to the branch until he was eyeball to eyeball with the worm. The worm stopped his movement and went very still. "I won't hurt you," said Gilbert. "I just want to be friends."

"Well," the worm said in a squeaky voice. "I'm trying to get to those nice leaves. It's almost lunch time, and I am hungry!"

"Oh, I see!" said Gilbert. "I like some leaves, grass, and clover. Do you like clover?"

The worm said, "Well, sometimes, but right now I've got to eat because I think I'm growing."

Gilbert asked, "What's your name?"

The worm replied, "Ryan, and what's yours?"

"My mommy and daddy call me 'Gilbert,'" he replied. "You're a strange looking worm because you've got legs, and a lot more than me. I've got four legs, and you've got six up front and six in the back."

"They help me to hold on to the branches and reach across twigs. I can even hold on to the leaf with my front legs while my back legs hold on to the branch."

"Wow!" said Gilbert. He watched as Ryan climbed higher and higher up on the branch.

The next day, Gilbert went looking for Ryan, and after searching for an hour, he found Ryan far up the briar patch. Gilbert called, "Ryan! Hey, Ryan! It's me, Gilbert! How are you today?"

Ryan looked down and saw his friend, and he slowly climbed down to where he could talk to Gilbert. "Well, I'm glad to see you," said Ryan in his squeaky voice.

"I'm okay, but I'm feeling sleepy, and I think pretty soon I'm going to find a nice place to take a nap."

"Oh, I take naps all the time!" said Gilbert. "Can I watch when you take your nap?"

Ryan said yes, and slowly, he climbed up to another branch and found a big, broad leaf. He slowly climbed underneath the leaf and carefully held onto the leaf with his front feet as he began to move his back end against the stem of the leaf. It wasn't long until Ryan had spun a strong web on the leaf, and then, after checking to see that it was securely attached, he started to spin a cocoon around him.

Gilbert watched Ryan for over an hour as he carefully covered his entire body in a silky, white blanket. It almost looked like fur, and after sniffing the air for a time, Gilbert hopped back to his home.

Day after day, Gilbert hopped over to where Ryan slept, and he would call, "Ryan! Hey, Ryan! Are you awake yet?" But there was no answer from Ryan. He never moved but stayed snug in his cocoon.

Then one day, when the sun was overhead, Gilbert hopped over to see if Ryan had awakened, and all he found was an empty cocoon. Ryan was gone! "Now, what happened to Ryan?" thought Gilbert. "Where did he go?" Just as Gilbert was ready to hop away, a beautiful butterfly came fluttering by and landed on Gilbert's nose.

"Hey, Gilbert, it's me!" said the butterfly. "It's Ryan, and I am grown up!"

"Wow!" Gilbert said, amazed. "Ryan, you turned into a beautiful butterfly, and you can fly!"

"Yes, I can!" said Ryan. "Let's play!"

Gilbert hopped around, and Ryan flew overhead. Ryan and Gilbert played together the rest of the day and for many days after that.

Gilbert Finds a Moving Rock

BY
POPPY

B y now you know that Gilbert is a mischievous little bunny rabbit who is always finding new things that only Mommy can explain to him.

But one day, as he carefully went out into the meadow, he spotted something very strange that he had never seen before in the grass.

It was a large rock, about the size of a helmet, and it was moving through the grass as if it was on an adventure.

Carefully, Gilbert crept up to it. He sniffed the air and then the rock to see if he recognized the smell.

It was nothing he had seen nor smelled before! The rock kept moving across the meadow at a steady pace.

Gilbert watched as a head and neck appeared from the front part of the rock. The head started to eat the grass that Gilbert also enjoyed.

Hey, maybe the rock was alive and a creature he hadn't seen before!

Gilbert went around to where the head had appeared, and quickly, the head withdrew into the rock, and a trap door shut tightly so Gilbert's nose couldn't sniff any odor from it.

Carefully, Gilbert extended his paw to touch the rock, and it didn't move at all but stayed still.

Now, Gilbert was puzzled! What was this thing? Can *you* guess what it was?

In a moment, the head came out, and little legs came out from the sides. The rock began to move again, and this time, Gilbert saw a little tail come out from the rear. The rock began to crawl away.

"Hey!" Gilbert said. "Where are you going?"

The rock stopped moving, and it spoke! "I'm hungry for nice clover. Do you know where I can get some?" asked the rock.

Gilbert replied, "Yes, I do! Just follow me!"

So Gilbert started hopping toward the clover patch that he enjoyed, and the rock followed him across the meadow.

As they traveled, Gilbert began to ask the rock a few questions. "Hey, what's your name? And what are you?"

"Why, I'm a box turtle!" replied the rock. "My name is William, but my friends call me 'Billie.' What is your name?"

Gilbert replied, "Gilbert, and I'm a rabbit."

"Let's be friends and eat some clover!"

Billie couldn't hop or move as fast as Gilbert, so they took their time crossing the meadow to get some clover. Every now and then, Billie would stop and take a bite of grass and slowly chew it before moving on.

The sun was getting higher in the sky, and it was getting warmer, so Gilbert hurried along as fast as he could, always looking at the sky for hawks or any danger.

Billie didn't seem to be afraid of anything, and he moved at a slow pace.

Gilbert asked Billie, "So why do you hide under a rock?"

Billie just laughed and said, "I carry my house on my back, and it protects me from danger and keeps me dry when it rains. But I do feel hot if the sun beats down on me, and when it gets cold, I feel sleepy and need to dig into the ground to stay warm."

They went past some sticker bushes, and Billie went over to them to look for any berries that may have sprouted. He found a luscious blackberry and began to eat it, but he asked Gilbert if he wanted a taste.

Gilbert went over and tried a small bite. It tasted sweet to him, but he preferred leaves more. Billie ate a few more berries, and Gilbert ate some leaves, and they enjoyed each other's company.

Gilbert heard his mother calling him, so he told Billie that he had to go home, but he would come back after answering his mother's call.

Gilbert carefully hopped back across the meadow, watching for danger, but he looked forward to seeing his new friend again soon.

Billie also kept moving toward the place Gilbert had told him about and looked forward to the taste of the clover.

He hoped Gilbert liked clover like he did.

What do you think?

Do only animals eat clover or do children like to eat clover or do children only like to eat fruit and vegetables?

What do you enjoy to eat?

We all eat a variety of things like fruit and vegetables so that we can grow big and strong. Our bodies need milk to make strong bone so we have to listen to our Mommies and eat what they tell us to.

We will then grow big and strong and be like our parents one day.

Rabbits only need green plants but boys and girls need a lot of other foods to grow so we need to listen to our Parents and eat what they tell us to so we can grow as well.

Let's grow up to be healthy people!

CPSIA information can be obtained
at www.ICGtesting.com
Printed in the USA
BVHW022300040422
633291BV00019B/919

9 781662 844492